THE
Late Loon

Written and Illustrated by
Dean Bennett

DOWN EAST BOOKS

ISBN (10-digit): 0-89272-730-6

ISBN (13-digit): 978-0-89272-730-8

Library of Congress Control Number: 2006928485

Design by Chilton Creative

Printed in China

OGP 5   4   3   2   1

DOWN EAST BOOKS

A division of Down East Enterprise, Inc.

Publisher of *Down East*, the Magazine of Maine

Book orders: 1-800-685-7962

www.downeastbooks.com

Acknowledgments

I thank John Richardson and Regina Webster for
giving me the idea for this story. They know all too well
the dangers loons face, for they—with their old beagle,
Jasper—have for many years lived in Maine's Allagash
Wilderness Waterway. I also thank my editor, Chris
Cornell, for his continued encouragement and guidance.
Finally, I especially thank Sheila, my wife and fellow loon
watcher, for her steadfast support. Together we have had
years of wildlife-watching pleasure, paddling the rivers
and lakes of Maine's north woods.

John and Reggie live with Jasper, their old beagle dog, on the shores of a big lake in northern Maine. One misty August morning they decide to launch their canoe and paddle down the lake shore.

As they enter a sheltered inlet, they hear a cry that sounds almost like a laugh—it's the alarm call of a loon. They see the loon swimming near the shore where tall marsh grass grows.

Today John and Reggie are going to hike to a nearby pond to check on a canoe they keep there. They paddle to shore, being careful not to get too close to the loon. Then, as Reggie starts to step on shore, Jasper suddenly jumps from the canoe! Fast as he can go, the old beagle runs up the shore toward the tall marsh grass. The loon on the lake begins to call even more loudly.

Curious, John and Reggie follow Jasper as he pushes through the marsh grass and finds a loon sitting motionless. Before they can get any closer, the bird slips into the water, and then they see it—the loon had been sitting on a nest with one greenish dark-brown egg!

Softly calling to Jasper, they back away quickly, leaving the nest undisturbed, but Reggie is worried. "This is much too late for loons to be incubating an egg," she says. "Loon eggs are supposed to hatch in June!"

John is worried, too. "By the time this young loon can fly, the lake is apt to be frozen over, and it will not be able to leave for the loons' winter fishing grounds along the coast," he says.

A couple of weeks later, in September, John and Jasper return to the inlet They see a loon swimming nearby and are careful to stay away from the loon nest as they step ashore. Then John hears Jasper bark. The dog is chasing a red fox near the loon nest! John walks up to check the nest and finds the egg still there.

Back at their cabin later that day, John tells Reggie, "It looked like a fox found the nest and its egg, but Jasper chased it away."

One day near the end of September, Reggie and Jasper are down on the dock by their camp, preparing to take a trip down the lake. As she picks up Jasper to put him into the boat, Reggie notices something at the upper end of the cove. It is a loon with a tiny, fuzzy chick riding on its back! The egg from the loon nest must have hatched just a few days ago. The parent loons have brought their new chick here to this cove because it is full of minnows and other small fish loons like to eat.

During the next few days, John and Reggie watch the tiny loon being fed. Sometimes the parent loon will lower itself in the water so the chick can swim off its back. When the chick is ready to go piggy-back again, the parent again lowers itself in the water, and the baby loon swims aboard. Not too many days go by, before they notice that it no longer rides at all. It still stays close to its parents, however.

Jasper, too, is fascinated by the loon family and often stands on the dock watching them.

As the end of October approaches, the birches, maples, and aspens in the surrounding forest lose their leaves and the landscape begins to look gray and empty around the camp. Winter is coming.

Out on the lake, the young loon is growing rapidly. Jasper, who likes being around the water, sometimes hears it making squeaks as it begs for food. Its parents answer with short, soft hoots.

One evening at sunset, as Jasper watches the loons fishing in the cove, a dark shadow suddenly passes over him. A huge bald eagle swoops down, headed directly for the baby loon!

The swoosh of the eagle's wings frightens Jasper, and he gives his loud beagle bark. Startled by the noise, the young loon dives to safety just before the eagle's talons rake the water's surface. It was a close call. Once again, Jasper has protected the loon chick.

November comes, and the days grow colder. Jasper finds a film of ice along the shore of the lake. Reggie and John have been seeing flocks of loons on the lake since October. Those loons soon fly off to the coast for the winter, but the loon family in Reggie and John's cove stays behind. Their young loon begin has begun to feed itself but it is still unable to fly.

In late November, it is time for John to pull his boats and canoes out of the water to store them for the winter. Jasper comes along to watch. As he works, John notices that now there are no loons anywhere on the lake. The last flocks are gone and everything is quiet.

"It looks like all the loons have left," he tells Reggie later. "I sure hope the young loon went, too."

December arrives and the cove freezes over. Down by the lake, John and Reggie are cleaning the cabins where guests will soon be staying when they come to the lake for ice fishing. Jasper goes down to the shore too. After a little while, Jasper and Reggie see a lone loon fishing at the edge of the ice at the mouth of the cove—the young loon did not leave with the others! Reggie worries that it may be in trouble.

Just a few nights later, the big lake in front of the camp freezes over completely. John, Reggie, and Jasper are awakened in early morning by the mournful wailing of the loon. They rush to the shore to find out what is happening.

There is the lone young loon in a small circle of open water surrounded by ice. It is swimming around and around, pecking at the edge of the ice to keep the opening from closing in completely. The opening is too small for it to get airborne. Loons need a long stretch of open water to take off.

Night after night, the loon's wailing goes on. John and Reggie can't sleep. They think about the poor loon all the time and are terribly worried. They try to think of some way to help the trapped bird, but the ice is too thin for them to walk across. It looks hopeless for the loon, and Jasper senses their discouragement and unhappiness.

Then one day Reggie notices that the temperature is becoming warmer. Several days of rain follow, and the ice on the lake begins to melt. When the rain stops, a high wind comes up. It blows fiercely all night, and strong gusts shake John and Reggie's cabin.

The next morning, they see patches of open water on the lake where the ice has broken up. With Jasper following, they rush down to the shore to see if the loon is still there. At first they see nothing. "The loon has flown away!" John says. They all feel relieved.

But then the loon appears. "No, it's still here. It must still be unable to fly," says Reggie sadly.

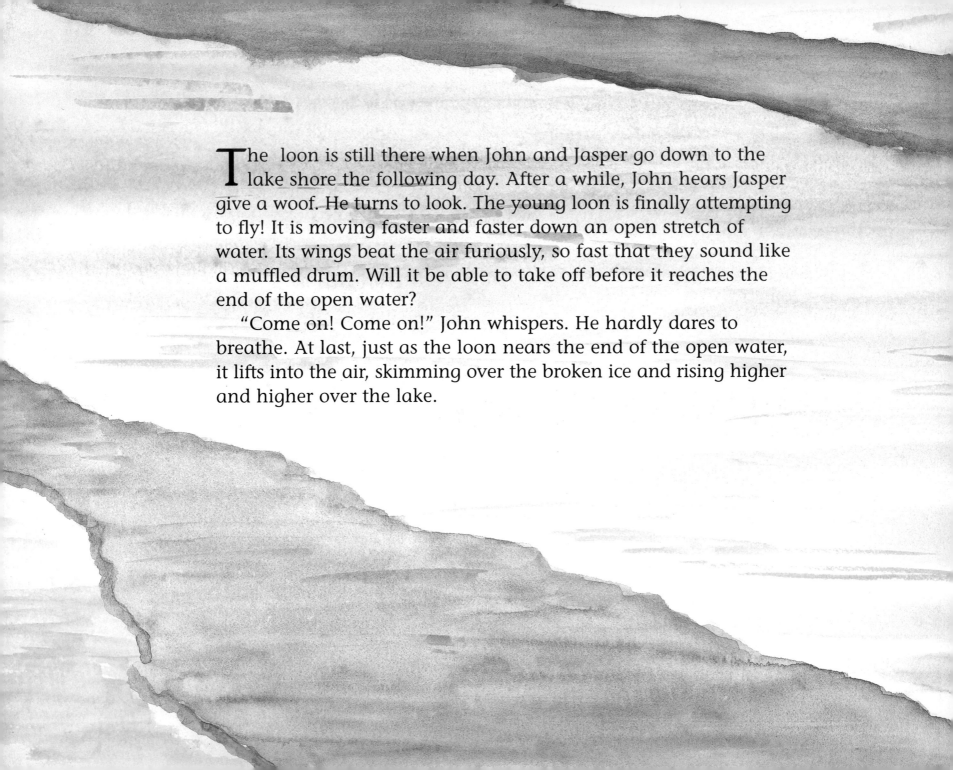

The loon is still there when John and Jasper go down to the lake shore the following day. After a while, John hears Jasper give a woof. He turns to look. The young loon is finally attempting to fly! It is moving faster and faster down an open stretch of water. Its wings beat the air furiously, so fast that they sound like a muffled drum. Will it be able to take off before it reaches the end of the open water?

"Come on! Come on!" John whispers. He hardly dares to breathe. At last, just as the loon nears the end of the open water, it lifts into the air, skimming over the broken ice and rising higher and higher over the lake.

"The loon made it. It has flown away!" shouts John as he runs back to the cabin. Jasper has to trot to keep up. Reggie sees them coming and hurries out of the cabin to join them, and all three turn to watch the loon fly out of sight.

Jasper feels a gentle pat on his back. "Your little loon is grown up now, Jasper," says Reggie, "and someday it may return."

AUTHOR'S NOTE

Although there is the chance that a
loon might be trapped by ice in late fall,
most of the dangers loons face come
from people. We can help protect loons
by staying away from their nesting
places, by not polluting their lakes and
ponds, and by retrieving fishing gear and
not using lead sinkers. Local conservation
groups and lake associations, libraries,
and the Internet are all good sources of
information about loons and what
you can do to help protect them.